ANNE BONNY

A LIFE OF DEFIANCE

HILMARJ TORGRIM

MANDOLIN PUBLISHING

Published by the Mandolin Publishing Group

Some names and characteristics of people mentioned have been changed, most events have been compressed. Randomly italicized words are for author emphasis only. While this story is based on the real life of the main character, it is a fictional story told through the perspective of the main character. Places, depictions, descriptions and names may have been changed for the sake of the story.

Anne Bonny: A Life of Defiance

Early Life (Uncertain Dates)

- Birth: Likely in Cork, Ireland, around 1697 (disputed)
- Illegitimate daughter of an attorney and his servant
- Raised unconventionally, possibly disguised as a boy
- Eventually emigrated to South Carolina with her family

Turning to Piracy (Early 1720s)

- Fled South Carolina with a pirate named James Bonny (possibly not a marriage)
- Joined Calico Jack Rackham's crew, dressing and fighting as a man
- Developed a romantic relationship with Mary Read (another woman disguised as a man)

The Revenge and the Rise to Notoriety (1720)

- Staged a mutiny and became captain of the Revenge
- Pillaged ships in the Caribbean alongside Mary Read and Blackbeard
- Became a legend for her fierceness and skill in battle

The Cursed Fort and a Deal with the Devil (1720)

- Led an expedition to a rumored Spanish stronghold
- Encountered a curse and a ghostly guardian
- Made a bargain to appease the spirit and break the curse

Facing Authority and a Pyrrhic Victory (1720)

- Returned to Nassau with a strange artifact but no gold
- Negotiated with Governor Rogers, offering the artifact and information
- Avoided the gallows but lost her captaincy and crew

Uncertain Fate (1720 onwards)

- Separated from Mary Read, captured by another pirate

- Sentenced to death for piracy but
  granted a reprieve due to pregnancy
- Disappearance from historical records –
  rumors of escape or a quiet life

Legacy

- Became a symbol of female defiance
  and piracy
- Her story continues to inspire and
  intrigue centuries later
- The truth behind her final days remains
  a mystery

Chapter 1

The salty spray stung Anne's face as she gripped the rail of the rickety sloop, the wind whipping her fiery red hair into a frenzy. Her knuckles shone white, the only splash of color against the drab browns and greys of her servant's garb. Below, the churning waves mirrored the turmoil in her heart.

Leaving everything she knew behind was a desperate gamble, but one she was forced to take. Her life in Charleston had soured, choked by the suffocating expectations of a proper lady. Marriage to a wealthy plantation owner loomed, a prospect as bleak as the swamps surrounding the city. Anne craved adventure, a life untamed, a life on the open sea.

The sloop, a ramshackle vessel named the "Sea Serpent," bobbed precariously in the unforgiving Atlantic. Captain Matthias, a wiry man with a weathered face and a single gold tooth glinting in his smile, barked orders at his ragtag crew. They were smugglers, barely a step above pirates, but to Anne, they were her ticket to freedom.

Their destination – Nassau, the infamous pirate haven in the Bahamas. It was a lawless den of cutthroats and scoundrels, a place where a woman, even one disguised as a boy with a chopped mane of hair and borrowed breeches, could disappear.

The journey was arduous, filled with the monotonous creak of the ship and the ever-present threat of storms. Anne spent her days learning the ropes, from hauling sails to navigating by the stars. Captain Matthias, gruff but surprisingly patient, saw the fire in her emerald eyes and the strength in her calloused hands. He saw a potential pirate, a soul yearning for the wild freedom of the sea.

One stifling night, as the moon cast an eerie glow on the water, Anne overheard a hushed conversation. The crew was plotting a raid on a Spanish galleon rumored to be laden with gold. Fear coiled in her stomach, but it was quickly overshadowed by a thrill, a taste of the life she craved. This was no mere smuggling run; it was piracy, a crime punishable by death. Yet, the thought of facing the hangman's noose seemed preferable to the suffocating life that awaited her on land.

As dawn painted the sky with streaks of orange and pink, Captain Matthias announced their change of course. Anne's heart hammered in her chest, a drumbeat for the adventure that lay ahead. She had crossed the point of no return. Anne Bonny, the dutiful servant, was gone. In her place stood Anne Bonny, the pirate-to-be, ready to face whatever storms, both literal and figurative, awaited her on the Isle of New Providence.

Chapter 2

Nassau bustled with a chaotic energy that both terrified and exhilarated Anne. The ramshackle port overflowed with pirates, their laughter and drunken brawls echoing off the weathered buildings. Women of ill repute hawked their wares with practiced smiles, while merchants with missing limbs and patched-up eyes hawked stolen goods. The air hung thick with the smell of rum, sweat, and the decay of the sea.

Matthias steered Anne through the teeming streets, his hand clamped firmly on her shoulder to prevent her from being swept away by the throng. He led her to a seedy tavern, the "Drunken Parrot," its sign swinging precariously in the hot Caribbean wind. Inside, a motley crew of pirates filled the dimly lit space, drinking, gambling, and swapping tales of daring exploits. Smoke from cheap tobacco filled the air, making Anne cough.

"This be Calico Jack Rackham," Matthias said, pushing her towards a broad-shouldered man with a flamboyant red beard and a feathered hat perched on his head. "He's the captain we'll be joining for the raid."

Calico Jack was everything Anne expected a pirate captain to be – loud, boastful, and reeking of stale rum. He eyed her with amusement, a smirk playing on his lips. "Matthias tells me you be a new recruit, lad. Got the stomach for a fight?"

Anne met his gaze, her jaw set firm. "I do, Captain."

A slow grin spread across Jack's face. "Good. We set sail at dawn."

The next few hours were a blur of frantic activity. Anne was outfitted with a cutlass and a brace of pistols, their weight unfamiliar but not unwelcome in her hands. She practiced drawing and firing, the sharp crack of the pistols echoing in the air. Though her muscles screamed in protest, a thrill coursed through her veins. This was real, this was dangerous, and it was exhilarating.

As the sun peeked over the horizon, casting an orange glow on the harbor, Anne boarded Jack's ship, the "Revenge." It was a far cry from the Sea Serpent, a larger, more imposing vessel with fearsome cannons lining its deck. The crew was a motley bunch – hardened veterans with missing limbs and scars etched into their faces, alongside younger men with reckless glint in their eyes. Anne, disguised in her boyish garb, felt a strange sense of belonging amongst these outcasts.

Finally, a lookout spotted their target on the horizon – a Spanish galleon, its white sails billowing in the breeze. A hush fell over the crew, replaced by a tense anticipation. Captain Jack slammed his fist on the table. "Time to claim our fortune, lads! Raise the Jolly Roger!"

The black flag with the skull and crossbones unfurled, a symbol of death and defiance. The air crackled with nervous energy as the Revenge changed course, heading straight towards the unsuspecting galleon. Anne took a deep breath, the taste of salt on her lips a stark contrast to the dryness in her mouth. The life she had craved was finally upon her, and with it, the first taste of battle.

Chapter 3

The roar of cannons shattered the morning calm as the Revenge bore down on the unsuspecting Spanish galleon. Anne felt a jolt of adrenaline surge through her as the first plume of smoke erupted from the enemy ship. In the chaos, Matthias shoved a loaded pistol into her hand. "Stay low, lad, and follow orders!"

Ducking behind the ship's railing, Anne joined a seasoned pirate named Blackheart, whose missing ear and tattooed skull on his arm spoke volumes of his experience. Blackheart barked orders, directing fire on the Spanish rigging, aiming to cripple their movement. The air was thick with the acrid smell of gunpowder and the deafening roar of cannons. Splinters flew as stray shots tore into the Revenge's wooden hull.

Suddenly, a deafening crack echoed through the deck. Blackheart cried out, clutching his shoulder, a bloodstain blooming on his tattered shirt. In a surge of primal rage, Anne pushed herself to her feet, adrenaline masking the fear threatening to consume her.

Raising the pistol, she took aim at the nearest Spanish sailor on the deck, ignoring the frantic scrambling of nearby crewmates who hadn't noticed her yet. With a white-knuckled grip, she squeezed the trigger. The pistol recoiled violently, the loud report almost drowned out by the surrounding cacophony. Through the smoke, she saw the Spanish sailor crumple to the deck.

A scream tore from her throat, a primal roar of defiance. It wasn't just the thrill of the kill, but a desperate need to prove herself, to belong amidst these battle-hardened pirates. She reloaded with shaking hands, her earlier training taking over on instinct. Blackheart, gritting his teeth against the pain, nodded at her in approval.

The battle raged on. The Spanish galleon, though surprised, wasn't about to go down without a fight. They returned fire, peppering the Revenge with cannonballs. Men on both sides fell, their screams lost in the din of battle.

Chaos erupted on the deck as the pirate crew, led by Calico Jack himself, grappled with the Spanish boarding party. Anne, fuelled by a newfound ferocity, joined the fray. Her cutlass felt surprisingly natural in her hand as she parried and slashed, her movements a blur of fury and newfound skill.

In a frenzy, she locked eyes with a burly Spanish soldier, his face contorted with rage. They clashed blades, the metallic clang echoing through the chaos. Anne, fueled by adrenaline, fought with a surprising strength and agility, surprising even herself. The fight went back and forth until she saw a chance, a flicker of vulnerability in the Spaniard's defense. With a swift movement, she disarmed him, her blade finding purchase in his shoulder with a sickening thud.

The Spaniard crumpled to the ground, a look of disbelief etched on his face. Anne stood panting, her clothes ripped and bloodied, but with a sense of exhilaration she had never known before. She was no longer just a disguised farm girl; she was Anne Bonny, the pirate.

But the battle was far from over. The Spanish fought with desperate tenacity, but the tide was turning in favor of the pirates. With a final roar,

Captain Jack himself disarmed the Spanish captain, forcing their surrender.

Exhausted but exhilarated, Anne surveyed the bloody scene. The deck was littered with the fallen from both sides, a grim reminder of the price of victory. Despite the carnage, a sense of accomplishment, a dark satisfaction, bloomed in her chest. She had not only survived her first battle, but thrived in it.

As the smoke cleared and the pirates began to secure their loot, Anne knew this was just the beginning. This life, dangerous and brutal as it was, was also fiercely free. And Anne Bonny, the pirate, had found her place within it.

Chapter 4

The aftermath of the battle was a blur of activity. The wounded were tended to, the dead cast overboard with a simple prayer, and the plundered bounty from the Spanish galleon inventoried with greedy glee. Gold coins clinked, silks shimmered, and the pungent aroma of exotic spices filled the air.

Exhausted but exhilarated, Anne slumped against the railing, watching the setting sun paint the sky with fiery hues. Her arm throbbed from a sword graze, but the ache was overshadowed by a strange sense of pride. She had tasted blood, fought with the ferocity of a lioness, and emerged a survivor, a victor.

"Well fought, lad," a gruff voice rumbled beside her. Blackheart, his injured shoulder bandaged, leaned against the railing, his single remaining eye twinkling with amusement.

"Thank you," Anne rasped, surprised by the warmth in his voice. Despite his fearsome appearance, Blackheart seemed to have taken her under his wing, impressed by her courage during the fight.

"You fought like a demon," he chuckled, spitting a stream of tobacco juice overboard. "Most seasoned pirates wouldn't have stood their ground against that Spaniard the way you did."

Anne felt a blush creep up her neck. "I just... I had to prove myself."

Blackheart snorted. "Prove yourself to whom? These scallywags?" He gestured at the crew, who were already celebrating their victory with a raucous drinking session. "They care little for your origins, lad. As long as you can fight and follow orders, you're one of them."

He studied her for a moment, his gaze piercing. "But I suspect there's more to you than meets the eye. You carry yourself differently. What brings a young lad like you to a life of piracy?"

Anne hesitated. Could she trust him? This gruff pirate, with his missing ear and scarred face, held a surprising amount of power over her.

Yet, something in his gaze, a flicker of understanding, made her choose to confide.

Taking a deep breath, she blurted out the story of her suffocating life in Charleston, the oppressive expectations, and her desperate escape. She spoke of her yearning for adventure, for a life lived on her own terms.

Blackheart listened intently, his expression unreadable. When she finished, he remained silent for a long moment, letting the waves lap against the hull fill the space between them.

Finally, he spoke, his voice low. "I understand more than you think, lad. Freedom is a powerful lure, and the sea offers a taste of it that few can resist."

He sighed, a hint of sadness in his voice. "But it also comes at a cost. This life, for all its excitement, is a brutal one. It's a constant dance with death, with the hangman's noose always looming."

He fixed her with a single, intense stare. "Are you sure you're prepared for what lies ahead?"

Anne met his gaze, her jaw set. "I am," she said, her voice ringing with conviction. "I'd rather die a pirate than live as a prisoner."

A slow smile spread across Blackheart's face, revealing a gold tooth glinting in the fading light. "Then welcome aboard, Anne Bonny, pirate."

For the first time since leaving Charleston, Anne felt a sense of belonging, a connection forged in the crucible of battle and shared secrets. The life of a pirate was a gamble, but she had thrown the dice, and her fate was now inextricably linked with the tumultuous waters of the Caribbean.

Chapter 5

Days turned into weeks as the Revenge cruised the turquoise waters of the Caribbean. The thrill of the recent battle faded, replaced by the monotony of daily life at sea. Anne found herself settling into a routine – mending sails, swabbing the deck, and learning the intricate art of navigation from the salty old sea dog known only as "Salty Pete."

At night, under the vast expanse of stars, she would join the crew around a crackling fire, listening to their raucous tales of past adventures and legendary pirates. She learned about Blackbeard, the fearsome pirate captain renowned for his cruelty and his fondness for setting alight slow-burning matches in his beard. Whispers of Captain Bartholomew Roberts, the swashbuckling Welshman known as "Black Bart," also reached her ears.

These tales fueled Anne's fire. She craved more than just the drudgery of sailing. She yearned for another skirmish, another chance to prove herself. But Captain Jack, despite being impressed by her fighting spirit, seemed hesitant to engage in another fight so soon. Resources were low, and the crew needed time to recuperate and sell their stolen goods.

One humid afternoon, while perched on the crow's nest, scanning the horizon for any sign of passing ships, Anne spotted a plume of smoke in the distance. Her heart pounded in her chest. Could it be another Spanish galleon, ripe for plundering?

She scrambled down the rigging, excitement bubbling within her. Rushing to Captain Jack, who was lounging in his cabin with a bottle of rum, she blurted out the news.

"Another ship, Captain! A hefty one by the looks of it!"

Jack raised an eyebrow, a flicker of interest sparking in his bloodshot eyes. He lumbered out of his cabin and climbed onto the deck, squinting towards the horizon.

"Could be a merchant vessel," he muttered, stroking his beard thoughtfully. "But it could also be a British warship. Those blasted navy dogs are always sniffing around, spoiling our fun."

A tense silence descended upon the deck. The crew, alerted by Anne's discovery, gathered around, their faces etched with anticipation. The sight of the approaching ship hung heavy in the air, a potential promise of riches or a harbinger of trouble.

Suddenly, a different kind of movement caught Anne's eye. A flash of red on the approaching vessel. Squinting further, she gasped. It wasn't a merchant ship, nor a British warship. It was the unmistakable Jolly Roger, a pirate flag flapping defiantly in the breeze.

Who could it be? A rival pirate crew? A potential ally? Anne felt a thrill course through her. Pirates, at least, weren't the enemy.

Captain Jack let out a booming laugh. "Well, well, well! Looks like we're not the only ones hunting for treasure in these waters."

He turned to his first mate, a wiry man named Charles Vane with a cruel glint in his eyes. "Prepare for battle, lads! We don't know who these pirates are, but one thing's for sure – this sea ain't big enough for two crews!"

The air crackled with anticipation. Anne gripped the hilt of her cutlass, her heart pounding with a mixture of fear and excitement. She was about to come face-to-face with another pirate crew. This wasn't just any encounter; it could be the start of a whole new adventure, a chapter yet unwritten in the wild and unpredictable story of Anne Bonny, the pirate.

Chapter 6

The approaching ship, revealed to be a sleek schooner, drew closer, its black flag snapping in the breeze. As the two vessels came within shouting distance, Anne craned her neck, straining to catch a glimpse of the other crew. A motley group of pirates lined the deck, a mix of men and women, some weathered and battle-scarred, others with youthful defiance in their eyes.

Suddenly, a woman with fiery red hair, her face painted with a fierce-looking skull, emerged from the crowd. A shiver ran down Anne's spine – a strange mix of recognition and a jolt of competitive spirit. This wasn't just any woman pirate; this woman seemed to command respect, her gaze as sharp as the cutlass strapped to her hip.

"Ahoy there!" the woman's voice boomed across the water, surprisingly strong and melodic. "Who sails the Revenge?"

Captain Jack, ever the showman, puffed out his chest and bellowed back. "Calico Jack Rackham at your service, and this fine vessel be the Revenge!"

"And I," the red-haired woman declared, raising her cutlass in a salute, "be Mary Read, captain of the 'Sea Hawk,' with a crew hungry for adventure!"

A low murmur of excitement rippled through the crew of the Revenge. Mary Read, a female pirate captain, was a legend whispered about in taverns and around campfires. The notion of meeting another woman who dared to defy convention filled Anne with a strange sense of kinship.

Captain Jack, however, seemed less enthused. He eyed Mary Read with suspicion, a scowl replacing his earlier bravado.

"Well, Captain Read," he said, his voice dripping with sarcasm, "what brings you to our neck of the woods? Don't tell me you're here to share stories and sing sea shanties."

Mary Read threw back her head and laughed, a bold, infectious sound that echoed across the waves. "Not at all, Captain Rackham. We, like you, are on the hunt for a bit of fortune."

She gestured towards a map clutched in her hand. "Word on the wind tells of a hidden Spanish galleon, laden with gold, wrecked on a deserted island just south of here."

A collective gasp arose from both crews. A Spanish galleon, a legendary wreck, the promise of untold riches… the tension on the deck crackled like static electricity.

Captain Jack's scowl deepened. "And you believe we'd just share the spoils with another crew? Don't be naive, woman."

Mary Read raised an eyebrow. "Naive? Captain Rackham, perhaps there's another way. Why risk bloodshed when we could combine our forces? Two crews are better than one in the face of the unknown, and who knows what dangers might lurk on that island?"

A thoughtful silence descended. Captain Jack stroked his beard, considering the options. Anne, however, couldn't contain her excitement. The idea of working alongside another female pirate, of proving her worth together, was an opportunity she couldn't miss.

Before Captain Jack could respond, Anne stepped forward, her voice ringing out across the water. "Captain Rackham," she said, her gaze resolute, "I think Mary Read has a point. Sharing the spoils is better than losing everything to some unknown danger."

A ripple of surprise passed through the crew, but Anne held their gaze. Even Blackheart, who had been observing her with a silent intensity, offered a small nod of approval.

Captain Jack studied Anne for a long moment. Finally, a sly grin spread across his face. "Well, well, Anne Bonny," he rumbled, "looks like you've got the spirit of a true pirate. Alright, Captain Read, your proposition has merit. Let's join forces and claim that Spanish gold together."

A cheer erupted from both crews, their earlier hostility replaced by the thrill of the hunt. Mary Read smiled, a genuine expression crinkling the corners of her eyes.

Anne felt a surge of pride. This wasn't just about the treasure; this was about forging an alliance, a bond between two women who defied the norms of their time on the untamed sea. The adventure, it seemed, was just getting started.

Chapter 7

The sun beat down mercilessly as the Revenge and the Sea Hawk sailed side-by-side towards the uncharted island marked on Mary Read's weathered map. The air was thick with anticipation, a mixture of excitement for the potential riches and trepidation for the dangers that might lurk on the unknown land.

Anne spent most of the day perched on the crow's nest, scanning the horizon for any sign of the wrecked Spanish galleon. Her heart pounded in her chest as the island finally emerged from the hazy distance, a jagged mass of emerald green against the turquoise canvas of the sea.

As they drew closer, a sense of foreboding hung heavy in the air. The island was desolate, devoid of any visible signs of life. The once-lush vegetation seemed to be choked by an unnatural darkness, the palm trees twisted and gnarled as if clawing at the sky.

"This place gives me the creeps," muttered Charles Vane, Captain Jack's first mate, his voice laced with suspicion.

Anne gripped the railing, a shiver running down her spine. The island did exude an unsettling aura, but it was the lure of the hidden treasure that fueled her resolve.

Finally, after navigating a treacherous coral reef, they found a sheltered cove where they could anchor both ships. Captain Jack and Mary Read, along with a small contingent from each crew, including Anne and Blackheart, disembarked onto the deserted beach.

The air on the island was thick and humid, filled with the buzzing of unseen insects. The vegetation crackled ominously as they ventured deeper into the island's heart, following the crude markings on the map.

Suddenly, Blackheart let out a low growl, his hand flying to his cutlass. A flash of movement caught Anne's eye – a group of figures emerging from the dense foliage. They were ragged men, clad in tattered clothes, their faces hardened with desperation.

"Pirates!" Charles Vane spat, drawing his pistol.

"Hold!" Mary Read boomed, her voice cutting through the tension. "They may not be hostile. Lower your weapons."

Anne watched cautiously as Mary Read cautiously approached the ragged figures, her hand resting on the hilt of her cutlass but her stance relaxed. The leader of the group, a burly man with a wild beard and a haunted look in his eyes, stepped forward.

"Who are you?" he rasped, his voice hoarse. "Have you come to steal what little we have left?"

Mary Read explained their quest for the Spanish galleon, her voice calm and reassuring. The man's face contorted in a mixture of anger and despair.

"There's no gold," he spat. "The island is cursed. It drove our captain mad, and the rest of us… we barely survived."

A wave of unease washed over Anne. If their information was true, then something far more sinister awaited them than a simple treasure hunt. But the thought of turning back, of leaving the promise of riches untouched, was unbearable.

Captain Jack stepped forward, a glint of avarice in his eyes. "Cursed or not, there's always something worth taking," he declared. "We'll find that gold, even if it means wrestling it from the devil himself!"

The pirate survivors looked at each other, their faces etched with fear and desperation. Mary Read, however, turned towards Captain Jack, her expression resolute.

"Perhaps there's another way," she said. "We can help these men escape this cursed island in exchange for their knowledge of the wreck."

Captain Jack scowled, but seeing the determination in Mary Read's eyes, he finally conceded. A shaky agreement was reached. They would guide the survivors back to Nassau, leaving this desolate island behind.

As they started their journey back to the beach, Anne couldn't help but feel a pang of disappointment. The thrill of the hunt had been replaced by a growing sense of unease. The island may not have held gold, but it had revealed a dark secret, a chilling reminder that the sea held more than just riches; it also held hidden dangers and terrifying curses.

However, Anne also witnessed something else that day - the unexpected compassion of Mary Read. The pirate captain, no less ruthless than her male counterparts, had shown a flicker of humanity, a willingness to help those in need. It was a side of a pirate's life that Anne hadn't considered, and it sparked a newfound respect for the woman who had defied expectations, just like her.

As they boarded the ships, the strange island fading into the distance, Anne knew their adventure was far from over. The hunt for treasure may have been thwarted, but the secrets of the Caribbean still beckoned. And Anne Bonny, the pirate, was ready for whatever challenges the sea might throw her way.

Chapter 8

The air in Nassau hung thick with the stench of rum, sweat, and desperation. The familiar sights and sounds of the pirate haven, once a source of excitement for Anne, now held a hint of disappointment. Their expedition to the cursed island had returned empty-handed, the promise of riches replaced by a chilling tale.

Captain Jack, ever restless, wasted no time in blowing his share of the meager spoils earned from ferrying the survivors back to Nassau on a drunken spree at the "Drunken Parrot." Anne, however, found herself drawn to a quieter tavern, a dimly lit establishment known as "The Rusty Cutlass."

The crowd here was different – a mix of seasoned pirates, weathered by years at sea, and young men with the glint of adventure in their eyes. Anne, her hair still cropped short and her face hidden beneath a worn tricorn hat, blended seamlessly into their midst.

Finding a seat in a shadowed corner, she nursed a tankard of ale, the bitterness mirroring her mood. A gruff voice broke the silence beside her.

"Rough seas out there, lad?"

Anne looked up to see a weathered pirate, his face a roadmap of wrinkles, his single remaining eye twinkling with amusement. He introduced himself as Ezra, a former quartermaster on Blackbeard's fearsome ship, the Queen Anne's Revenge.

Anne found herself drawn into conversation, sharing her tale of the cursed island and their disappointment. Ezra listened intently, his one eye glinting with a knowing light.

"Cursed islands are dime a dozen in these waters," he chuckled, his voice gravelly. "But there's always truth buried beneath the tall tales."

He leaned closer, his voice dropping to a conspiratorial whisper. "You wouldn't happen to have a copy of that map, would you?"

Anne's heart skipped a beat. The map, useless for finding gold, might hold more significance after all. "Maybe," she said cautiously. "Why do you ask?"

Ezra took another sip of his ale, his single eye locking with hers. "There's whispers, lad, of a hidden cove, untouched by whatever curse plagued that island. A cove filled with Spanish treasure, shipwrecked years ago. Captain might have dismissed it as sailor's yarn, but…"

He trailed off, leaving the sentence hanging in the air. Anne's pulse quickened. Could this be a second chance? A chance to redeem their failed expedition and finally claim a piece of pirate legend?

"But what about the curse?" Anne asked, her voice barely above a whisper.

Ezra shrugged. "Cursed or not, there's always a way for a clever pirate. Besides," he winked, "having a woman like you by my side might just ward off any evil spirits."

A slow smile spread across Anne's face. Maybe this gruff old pirate wasn't so bad after all. Here was an opportunity, a secret whispered in a darkened tavern, a chance to rewrite the narrative of their failed mission.

With a newfound spark of excitement, Anne glanced towards the "Drunken Parrot" across the way. There, Captain Jack was likely still drowning his sorrows. A mischievous glint entered her eye. Perhaps it was time for Anne Bonny, the pirate, to make a move of her own.

CHAPTER 9

The air buzzed with the bawdy shantals spilling out of the Drunken Parrot. Anne stood across the street, the worn tricorn pulled low, watching Captain Jack through the haze of rum and laughter. Disappointment gnawed at her. He wouldn't entertain the idea of a second expedition, especially guided by a mere "cabin boy" like her.

Anger simmered under the surface. She wouldn't let this opportunity slip through her fingers. But how to convince, or perhaps… persuade, a drunken pirate captain?

A mischievous plan hatched in her mind. Glancing toward the dock where the Revenge lay anchored, she saw Blackheart tinkering with the rigging. He was loyal, distrustful of Captain Jack's leadership, and perhaps, just perhaps, open to a change.

With newfound resolve, Anne slipped into the shadows, her boots silent on the cobbled streets. Reaching the docks, she found Blackheart engrossed in his work. "Blackheart," she whispered.

He startled, his hand instinctively going to his cutlass, then relaxed upon recognizing her. "Anne Bonny," he rumbled, his voice low. "What brings you here at this ungodly hour?"

"The chance for a real adventure, Blackheart," she declared, her voice filled with a fire that surprised even her. She quickly laid out her plan, the whispers overheard in the Rusty Cutlass, and the possibility of the untouched cove.

Blackheart listened intently, stroking his beard thoughtfully. A flicker of interest sparked in his single eye. "Intriguing, lad," he finally conceded. "But how do we convince the crew, let alone wrestle control from Captain Jack?"

"We let them see the Captain for who he is," Anne said, a glint of steel in her voice. "A drunken fool more interested in rum than riches."

Together, they formulated a plan. Blackheart would subtly stir up discontent amongst the crew, reminding them of the meager spoils from the last mission and Captain Jack's wasteful spending. Anne, disguised in the shadows, would anonymously leak word of the potential treasure trove.

The plan unfolded through the next few days. The once-festive crew grew sullen, grumbling about Captain Jack's leadership and their empty pockets. Rumors of a hidden treasure spread like wildfire, whispered conversations fueling frustration and a growing thirst for adventure.

Finally, under the cloak of a moonless night, Anne set her part of the plan in motion. With a piece of charcoal, she scrawled a message on the mainmast, large and clear in the morning light: "Follow the true leader. Hidden treasure awaits."

The next morning, the sight of the message on the mast caused an uproar. Captain Jack, still bleary-eyed from his drunken stupor, stumbled onto the deck to face a mutinous crew, Blackheart standing at the forefront.

"What's the meaning of this?" Captain Jack roared, his voice thick with hangover and confusion.

Blackheart stepped forward, his voice firm. "The crew has lost faith, Captain. We seek a fortune, not another night spent at the bottom of a rum bottle."

A wave of agreement rippled through the crew. Anne, her heart pounding in her chest, held her breath.

Seizing the moment, Blackheart gestured towards the disguised figure leaning against the railing. "And it seems we have a leader who promises us both."

All eyes turned towards Anne. She slowly straightened, her tricorn falling back, revealing her face to the bewildered crew. "I offer you a chance, a true pirate's adventure," she declared, her voice ringing out with surprising authority. "A chance at riches beyond our wildest dreams."

Silence descended upon the deck. The crew stared at her, surprised but not completely unwilling. Anne, adrenaline coursing through her veins, met their gazes one by one.

"Join me," she continued, her voice rising with conviction, "and together we'll claim our destiny! We'll be the ones who rewrite the legends of the Caribbean!"

A low murmur arose from the crew. Discontent morphed into a spark of excitement.

Blackheart, with a silent nod of approval, drew his cutlass and raised it towards the moon. The men, with a roar of approval, followed suit.

A mutiny had taken place, a gamble played under the cloak of darkness. Anne Bonny, the once-disguised cabin boy, now stood as the leader, ready to embark on a perilous quest guided by a whispered secret and her own unyielding spirit.

Chapter 10

The rising sun cast an orange glow on the deck of the Revenge as the crew scrambled to obey Anne's orders. Gone was the lethargy of the previous days, replaced by a fervent energy. Blackheart, now Anne's first mate, barked instructions with a newfound authority, his loyalty towards the new captain shining in his single eye.

Anne, clad in a stolen captain's coat that hung loosely on her slender frame, stood at the helm, a mix of excitement and trepidation warring within her. This wasn't just a gamble; it was a rebellion. She, a woman, had defied the established order and taken command of a hardened pirate crew. Would they follow her lead? Would they trust her to navigate them through uncharted waters and potential dangers?

As if sensing her doubts, Blackheart placed a calloused hand on her shoulder. "They wouldn't have chosen you, lass," he said, his voice low, "if they didn't believe you had the fire in your belly. Now, show them why."

Anne took a deep breath, her gaze settling on the tattered map clutched in her hand. The scribbled marks and faded ink held the key to their fortune, or perhaps, their doom. The whispers of a hidden cove, untouched by the curse that plagued the island, fueled her determination.

Days blurred into weeks as the Revenge sailed south, guided by the unreliable map and the whispers they'd overheard in the Rusty Cutlass. The crew, a motley bunch of hardened sailors and hungry young pups, grew restless under the relentless sun. Tensions simmered, fueled by dwindling supplies and the ever-present possibility of failure.

One sweltering afternoon, frustration boiled over. A hulking brute named Redbeard, known for his fiery temper, confronted Anne. "This is a fool's errand, Captain!" he bellowed, his face contorted in rage. "There's no treasure here, just another cursed island to swallow us whole!"

Other voices joined in the chorus of discontent. Anne held her ground, her voice unwavering despite the rising tide of doubt. "We don't turn back now," she declared, her eyes flashing with defiance. "We persevere. The reward will be worth the risk."

Suddenly, a lookout in the crow's nest let out a shout. "Land ahoy!"

A collective gasp arose from the deck. Hope, flickering like a dying ember, rekindled in their eyes. Anne's heart hammered in her chest. Could it be? Could they finally be at their destination?

As they drew closer, the island revealed itself. Unlike the previous one, this one was lush and inviting, fringed with white sand beaches and vibrant greenery. But a cautious tension still hung in the air. Was this a haven or a trap?

"We approach with caution," Anne ordered, her gaze sweeping over the crew. "Blackheart, take a small scouting party ashore. We need to know what we're dealing with before we set foot on that land."

Blackheart nodded curtly, his one eye gleaming with a mixture of apprehension and excitement. He handpicked a team, including the ever-grumbling Redbeard, and lowered a boat into the turquoise waters.

Anne watched them disappear towards the island, a knot of anxiety tightening in her stomach. They were close, tantalizingly close, to the potential fulfillment of their daring gamble. But the whispers of the curse lingered in her mind, a chilling reminder that the greatest treasures often come at the steepest price.

As the sun dipped below the horizon, painting the sky in hues of orange and purple, the scouting party returned. Blackheart's face, normally stoic, was etched with a mixture of awe and trepidation.

"Captain," he called out, his voice hoarse with excitement, "there's no curse here. Just a hidden cove, exactly as described in the map. And within it…" he paused, a dramatic flourish in his voice, "a ship. A Spanish galleon, half-buried in the sand, but… overflowing with treasure."

A cheer erupted from the crew, a cacophony of joy and relief. Anne's gamble had paid off. They had found their fortune. For now, at least, the rebellion that had propelled her into the role of captain seemed justified. But the real test, she knew, was yet to come. Claiming the treasure was one thing, escaping the island and navigating back to Nassau, a haven for pirates, was another.

The night hummed with anticipation. The crew, their doubts momentarily forgotten, celebrated their imminent success. Anne, however, stood alone at the helm, the weight of responsibility settling heavy on her shoulders. Leadership, she realized, wasn't just about barking orders and wielding a cutlass. It was about making tough decisions, anticipating dangers, and ensuring the survival of her crew.

As she gazed at the star-studded sky, a sense of determination solidified within her. She wasn't just Anne Bonny, the woman who defied expectations. She was Anne Bonny, captain of the Revenge, and she would lead them not just to riches, but back to the safety of Nassau, her legend etched not in whispers, but in the bold strokes of a pirate queen.

CHAPTER 11

The dawn broke over a scene of frantic activity. The beach teemed with pirates, their laughter and shouts echoing off the lush greenery. Shovels clanged against wood as they unearthed the half-buried Spanish galleon, its once-proud masts now mere skeletal fingers reaching towards the sky.

Anne, clad in her borrowed captain's coat, her sleeves rolled up to reveal the callouses forming on her hands, directed the operation with a newfound confidence. Blackheart, ever vigilant, patrolled the perimeter, ensuring no unwanted eyes stumbled upon their treasure trove.

Hours melted into a blur as chests overflowing with gold coins, silver goblets, and shimmering jewels were hauled onto the beach. The sight of the glittering bounty fueled the crew's excitement, but a sliver of unease gnawed at Anne.

Redbeard, his usual scowl replaced by a manic grin, hefted a chest filled with gold coins, his eyes gleaming with avarice. "This is enough for a lifetime, Captain!" he bellowed, his voice thick with greed.

Anne felt a pang of apprehension. The wealth they were amassing was a double-edged sword. It could solidify her leadership, but it could also breed dissent.

"We haven't finished yet," she said firmly. "There could be more hidden within the wreck itself."

A cheer went up, and the crew, their enthusiasm rekindled, scrambled towards the gaping hole they had created in the galleon's hull. Blackheart, who had been observing the scene with a thoughtful frown, approached Anne.

"Something troubles you, Captain?" he asked, his voice low.

Anne hesitated, then confided her worries. "The treasure can be a curse as much as a blessing. We need to secure it, but also keep the crew in line."

Blackheart nodded in agreement. "Perhaps we should make an example," he said, his voice grim. "Let them see what happens when greed takes hold."

His suggestion hung heavy in the air. Anne knew it was a gamble, but sometimes a firm hand was needed to maintain order, especially on a ship where loyalty could be as fleeting as the wind.

Suddenly, a strangled cry pierced the air. They spun around to see a young pirate named Billy, his face pale with terror, stumbling back from the galleon's interior.

"Redbeard!" he stammered, pointing a trembling finger towards the wreck. "He... he's trying to take a whole chest for himself!"

A wave of anger washed over Anne. Her worst fears were coming true. Just as quickly, however, a cold sense of calculation took hold.

"Blackheart," she said, her voice hard, "you know what to do."

Blackheart, with a grim nod, disappeared into the wreck. Moments later, the sound of a struggle erupted from within, followed by a string of curses. Blackheart emerged, dragging a struggling Redbeard behind him.

Redbeard, his face contorted in rage, sputtered accusations of betrayal. But the crew, witnessing the attempted theft, erupted in jeers and catcalls.

Anne stood before them, her gaze unwavering. Here was her chance. "Redbeard," she declared, her voice ringing out, "you have threatened the good of the crew for personal gain. That is a crime punishable by death."

A gasp rippled through the crowd. This was a decision unlike any she had made before. But she needed to establish her authority, to show that defiance wouldn't be tolerated.

Blackheart unsheathed his cutlass, its blade glinting in the morning sun. Redbeard, his bravado gone, looked around desperately for support, but found none.

With a deep breath, Anne intervened. "However," she continued, the words tasting like ash in her mouth, "you will not die. You will be marooned on this very island, a reminder of what happens when greed overshadows loyalty."

The crew went silent, the harsh sunlight reflecting in their eyes. It wasn't a death sentence, but it held a different kind of terror – isolation and the unknown dangers of the island. Redbeard, his face ashen, was dragged away, his defiant screams swallowed by the rustling of leaves.

The incident cast a dark shadow over their success. As the sun began its descent, painting the sky in hues of orange and red, the last of the treasure was secured on board the Revenge. A heavy silence hung in the air, broken only by the rhythmic creaking of the ship and the mournful call of unseen birds.

Anne stood by the helm, a weight far heavier than gold settling on her shoulders. Leadership, she realized, was a messy business. It demanded not just courage but also the capacity to make difficult choices.

But as she gazed at the horizon, the wind whipping at her hair, a spark of defiance ignited within her. She had weathered the storm, asserted her authority, and secured their fortune. Now, the real challenge awaited – navigating back to Nassau with a crew potentially fractured by greed and the ever-present threat of those who sought pirate riches.

"Set sail for Nassau!" she commanded, her voice ringing out with newfound resolve. The crew, their faces a mixture of fear and respect, scrambled to obey. They had a captain who was more than just a woman disguised as a man; they had a leader who wouldn't hesitate to make tough calls, and one who, perhaps, understood the true price of treasure a little too well.

As the Revenge cut through the turquoise water, leaving the deserted island and the marooned Redbeard behind, the sun dipped below the horizon, casting an ominous glow over their path. The journey back to Nassau promised to be anything but smooth sailing. Rumors of their success, whispers carried on the wind, might attract unwanted attention from rival pirates or the relentless pursuit of the British Navy.

But for now, Anne Bonny, captain of the Revenge, held the helm, her eyes fixed on the distant star that guided them home. She wasn't just returning with a ship laden with treasure; she was returning as a legend in the making – the woman who defied expectations, led a mutiny, and dared to claim her place at the helm of a pirate ship. The Caribbean, treacherous and unpredictable, awaited their return, and Anne Bonny, the pirate queen, was ready to face whatever storms it might bring.

Chapter 12

The days bled into a blur of endless blue skies and churning whitecaps. The crew, their initial excitement dampened by the harsh reality of long hours at sea, grew restless. The specter of Redbeard, marooned on the deserted island, served as a constant reminder of Captain Bonny's ruthlessness, keeping dissent in check but casting a pall over their victory.

One sweltering afternoon, the lookout's cry shattered the monotonous routine. "Ship ahoy! But not friendly!"

Anne rushed to the deck, her heart pounding against her ribs. A black flag with a skull and crossbones snapped lazily in the breeze, its owner unmistakable - the notorious Captain Calico Jack Rackham, the man whose ship she'd commandeered to become a pirate herself.

"Well, well," Rackham's voice boomed through a speaking trumpet, a sneer evident even at a distance. "Looks like our little cabin boy has grown some teeth."

Anne gripped the railing, a wave of anger and frustration washing over her. Rackham, with his flamboyant clothing and drunken swagger, represented everything she had defied.

"Stand down, Captain Rackham!" she shouted back, her voice surprisingly steady. "The Revenge is under my command now."

Rackham's laughter echoed across the water. "So the rumors are true. The cabin boy fancies himself a captain, eh? But a stolen ship won't save you from what's coming, Bonny."

He signaled his crew, their cannons roaring to life. The Revenge, caught unprepared, shuddered under the impact of the first volley. Anne, adrenaline surging through her veins, barked orders, directing the crew to return fire.

The battle raged, a deafening symphony of cannons and screams. Blackheart, ever the tactician, maneuvered the Revenge with surprising skill, dodging the worst of Rackham's attack. Anne, at the helm, watched the chaos unfold, a cold calculation forming in her mind.

They were outnumbered, outgunned. A head-on fight would be a disaster.

"Blackheart!" she yelled, the wind whipping her words away. "Prepare to ram!"

Blackheart's single eye widened, but he nodded curtly. The maneuver was risky, but it might be their only chance.

With a battle cry that echoed across the waves, Anne steered the Revenge towards Rackham's ship, the Queen Anne's Revenge. The crew, sensing their captain's desperation, put their backs into it, increasing the speed.

The impact was like hitting a wall. The Revenge shuddered violently, its mast groaning precariously. On the Queen Anne's Revenge, chaos erupted as sailors were thrown off their feet.

Using the momentary confusion, Anne ordered a retreat. Her ship, though heavily damaged, was still afloat. Rackham, cursing furiously, was not in a position to pursue.

As the Revenge limped away, the battered crew erupted in cheers. They had survived, thanks to their Captain's daring maneuver. But Anne felt no elation, only a gnawing worry.

News of their success, and the mutiny, would have reached Nassau by now. Governor Woodes Rogers, known for his ruthless pursuit of pirates, would be waiting for them. Their hard-earned fortune might not buy them the freedom they craved.

Nassau, once a haven, loomed on the horizon, a dark silhouette against the setting sun. As they sailed closer, the familiar ramshackle buildings and bustling docks seemed to hold a new, ominous air.

Anne stood at the helm, a bittersweet taste in her mouth. They had defied the odds, claimed their treasure, and earned the respect of their crew. But the real test of her leadership, she knew, was just beginning. Would Nassau offer them a pardon or a noose?

Chapter 13

The battered hull of the Revenge creaked in protest as it limped into Nassau harbor. The once-festive atmosphere Anne remembered was replaced by a tense silence. The normally bustling docks lay deserted, save for a lone figure standing stiffly at the pierhead: Woodes Rogers, the Governor of Nassau, his face a mask of disapproval.

Anne's heart pounded in her chest. The whispers she'd feared had reached him – whispers of mutiny, stolen ships, and a fortune waiting to be claimed. Her gamble, returning to Nassau instead of seeking a secluded haven, felt heavier with each passing moment.

"Captain Bonny," Governor Rogers boomed, his voice laced with disdain. "An impressive return, considering the rumors that preceded you."

Anne met his gaze, her jaw set firm. "Governor Rogers," she countered, her voice surprisingly steady. "We come seeking a pardon, not punishment."

Rogers scoffed. "A pardon for mutiny and piracy? You must be delusional, lass."

"We have information," Blackheart interjected, stepping forward for the first time. "Information that can be valuable to the Crown."

Rogers' eyebrows shot up in surprise. Intrigue flickered in his cold eyes. "Information of what nature?"

Blackheart glanced at Anne, a silent communication passing between them. This was their hail Mary, a gamble built on the whispers they'd overheard on their previous expedition.

"Information about a hidden Spanish stronghold," Blackheart said, his voice low. "A stronghold rumored to be brimming with riches, untouched by pirate hands."

Rogers' gaze narrowed. The allure of untold wealth was a powerful motivator, even for a man known for his rigidity. "How do I know this isn't another pirate's tall tale?"

"We offer proof," Anne said, a steely glint in her eye. "We retrieved a map from the cursed island – a map that might hold the key to this hidden treasure."

Governor Rogers pursed his lips, his gaze flickering between Anne and the battered ship she now commanded. He knew they were desperate, but were they desperate enough to fabricate such a tale?

Silence stretched, thick and suffocating, until Rogers finally spoke. "Very well," he said, his voice gruff. "Show me this map. If it proves genuine, we can discuss a… mutually beneficial arrangement."

Relief washed over Anne, a wave that nearly made her legs buckle. They weren't out of the woods yet, but they had sparked a flicker of interest. However, the map itself was unreliable, leading them on a wild goose chase before. It was a gamble, but one they had to take.

Blackheart hurried below deck, returning moments later with the worn piece of parchment. Rogers' expression remained unreadable as he examined the faded markings and cryptic symbols.

"This looks... promising," he conceded after a long pause. "But it requires verification. I suggest you lead an expedition under the Crown's flag, locate this stronghold, and offer a significant portion of the recovered treasure as... reparations."

Anne's stomach churned. Leading an expedition for the very government they'd defied was a bitter pill to swallow. Yet, it was a path to freedom, a way to escape the noose and perhaps even build a legitimate life.

"We accept your terms, Governor," she said, her voice betraying none of the turmoil within.

A ghost of a smile played on Rogers' lips. "Excellent. Your crew will be compensated for their 'services,' and your past transgressions... might be overlooked." He paused, his gaze lingering on Anne. "Captain Bonny. You've proven to be a bold leader. Let's hope you can lead as well for the Crown as you have for your own... interests."

Anne, her pirate spirit momentarily caged, met his gaze head-on. The future remained uncertain, but one thing was clear – her adventure, fueled by rebellion and a thirst for freedom, had taken a surprising turn. Now, she was a pirate captain sailing under a different flag, a woman playing a dangerous game with the very authorities she'd once defied. The journey to Nassau had brought them a reprieve, but the true test, she knew, awaited them beyond the horizon – a test that would define not just their freedom, but perhaps, their very legacy.

CHAPTER 14

The once-proud Revenge, now sporting a fresh coat of paint and the Crown's flag flapping dejectedly in the breeze, set sail with a crew of mixed emotions. Some, like Mary Read, a new recruit with a fiery spirit that mirrored Anne's own, saw it as an opportunity to prove themselves, to be more than just pirates. Others, like the ever-grumbling Redbeard, who had been miraculously "rescued" from the deserted island by a conveniently passing merchant ship (thanks to a hefty bribe from Anne), grumbled about working for the very authorities they'd spent their lives evading.

Anne, grappling with her own conflicting feelings, stood at the helm. They were no longer pirates, not truly. They were privateers, sanctioned by the Crown, sailing towards an uncertain future. The map, clutched tightly in her hand, felt more like a symbol of their deal with the devil than a guide to riches.

Days bled into weeks, the vastness of the Caribbean a constant reminder of their dependence on the unreliable map. The crew grew restless, the whispers of mutiny that had once threatened Anne now aimed at Blackheart, whose loyalty was questioned under the Crown's banner.

One particularly scorching afternoon, a lookout's cry pierced the oppressive silence. "Land ahoy!"

Hope flickered in their eyes. Could this be it? The culmination of their gamble with Governor Rogers?

As they drew closer, a foreboding feeling settled over Anne. The island wasn't the lush paradise depicted in the rumors. This one was desolate, shrouded in a perpetual mist, skeletal trees clawing at the sky like skeletal fingers reaching from a watery grave.

"Looks more like a place cursed than blessed with riches," Redbeard muttered, voicing the apprehension lurking in the hearts of many.

But there it was, nestled in a cove shrouded in mist – a fort, its once-imposing walls now crumbling, the Spanish flag hanging limp and lifeless. This was it, the fabled Spanish stronghold.

Tension hung heavy in the air as they lowered the anchor. Blackheart, ever cautious, suggested a scouting party before venturing ashore. Anne, despite an unsettling feeling that gnawed at her gut, agreed.

Hours passed, filled with an agonizing silence that was broken only by the crashing of waves against the rocky shore. Just as worry began to gnaw at Anne's resolve, a figure stumbled out of the mist, his face pale and eyes wild. It was William, the young pirate who had been part of the initial scouting party.

"The fort… it's empty," he stammered, his voice raspy. "But not untouched. Skeletons… everywhere. And whispers… whispers of a curse."

A cold dread washed over Anne. The whispers they'd heard, dismissed as pirate lore, were starting to feel unnervingly real.

Blackheart, his single eye narrowed, stepped forward. "Seems this island holds its own secrets, Captain."

Anne gazed at the skeletal figure of the fort, the mist swirling around it like a shroud. This wasn't just a quest for treasure anymore. It was a desperate attempt to escape a curse that seemed to follow them like a relentless shadow.

"We came for treasure," Anne finally declared, her voice echoing across the now-still water. "But we may find ourselves fighting for survival instead."

And with that, taking a deep breath and drawing her cutlass, Anne led her crew towards the mist-shrouded fort, the whispers of a curse a haunting premonition in the salty air.

Chapter 15

The mist clung to them like a shroud as they ventured into the fort. The air hung heavy with the smell of decay and a sense of forgotten battles. Cobwebs draped the crumbling archway, and broken cannons lay scattered like fallen teeth. The place felt more like a tomb than a treasure trove.

Cautiously, weapons drawn, they moved through the echoing halls. Skeletons, bleached white by the sun, sat slumped against walls, their empty sockets staring sightlessly. It was a chilling tableau, a stark reminder of the fate that might claim them all.

Suddenly, a loud clang echoed from a room ahead. Blackheart, ever vigilant, gestured for silence and crept forward, followed by Anne and a small contingent. Peeking through the broken archway, their eyes widened in surprise.

The room was packed with chests, overflowing with gold coins, shimmering jewels, and priceless artifacts. It was a treasure hunter's dream, a pirate's paradise. But a disquieting silence hung over the room, broken only by the dripping of unseen water.

"Fortune favors the bold," Redbeard muttered, pushing his way through the group. He lunged towards a chest, his eyes gleaming with avarice.

Before he could even touch it, a ghostly moan filled the room. A spectral figure materialized in the air before them, clad in faded Spanish garb, clutching a chest to his spectral form. Its face, a mask of fury and despair, seemed to lock onto Redbeard.

"This... this is mine!" the ghost shrieked, its voice an echoing rasp. "Mine by right, earned with blood and sweat! Not yours for the taking!"

Redbeard, his face paling, stumbled back. The rest of the crew stared in stunned silence. This was no ordinary treasure; it was cursed, bound to the restless spirit of its former guardian.

The ghost turned its attention to Anne, its spectral form shimmering with an eerie luminescence. "You... with the fire in your eyes," it rasped, "you understand the value of what is earned, not stolen. Do you seek this treasure? Then prove yourself worthy!"

A trapdoor in the center of the room opened with a groan, revealing a dark abyss. The ghost pointed towards it with a skeletal hand. "Descent into darkness. Bring me an artifact from the depths, a true test of courage and not just greed. If you succeed, the treasure might be yours. Fail… and join the ranks of the restless."

Anne's heart pounded in her chest. This was a gamble unlike any she had faced before. But backing down meant not just losing the treasure, but facing Governor Rogers' wrath.

She met the ghostly gaze head-on. "We accept your challenge," she declared, her voice ringing with newfound determination. "Half of my crew will stay to guard the treasure, the others will follow me. Blackheart, you're with me."

Blackheart nodded curtly, his single eye unwavering. Redbeard, however, let out a cry of protest. "But Captain, this is madness! We could be rich without risking our lives!"

Anne ignored him. Her gaze swept over the crew, seeking volunteers. A handful, including the fiery Mary Read, stepped forward, their faces etched with a mixture of fear and determination.

"Very well," the ghost rasped, a hint of respect in its voice. "May courage be your shield and good fortune your blade. The answers you seek lie below."

With a final piercing moan, the ghost dissipated, leaving behind a chilling silence. Anne glanced at the dark maw of the trapdoor, a knot of unease twisting in her stomach. This was more than just a quest for treasure; it was a test of her leadership, a gamble with their very lives.

Taking a deep breath, Anne drew her cutlass and approached the trapdoor. "Stay on guard here," she ordered the remaining crew. "We'll find out what lies beneath this cursed fort, and hopefully, a way to break its hold."

With Blackheart by her side and the brave souls who followed her, Anne lowered herself into the darkness, the unknown depths beckoning, promising answers and perhaps, a way to escape the clutches of the curse. As the heavy trapdoor slammed shut above them, Anne knew that the greatest treasure they might find wouldn't be gold or jewels, but a way

to break free from the cycle of greed and the
vengeful spirits it unleashed.

Chapter 16

The descent into the darkness was a suffocating journey. Damp air clung to their skin, and the only sounds were the rhythmic scraping of their boots on rough stone steps and the ragged gasps of their breaths. Even Blackheart, usually stoic, seemed to have a flicker of unease in his solitary eye.

After what felt like an eternity, they landed on a solid but uneven surface. Anne drew her flintlock pistol, the only light source apart from a small lantern they had brought. The chamber they stood in felt like a forgotten tomb – dust-covered chests and urns lay scattered on the floor, and cobwebs draped decaying tapestries on the walls.

The air grew thick with the stench of decay, and a low, rhythmic dripping echoed from somewhere within the chamber. It was a place devoid of life, a stark contrast to the sun-drenched fort above.

"What are we looking for, Captain?" Mary Read whispered, her voice barely a tremor in the stifling silence.

Anne scanned the room, searching for any clues the ghost might have left behind. A glint in the dim lantern light caught her eye – a weathered inscription carved into a nearby wall. Squinting closer, she deciphered the faded Spanish words: "Heart of the Sea, where shadows sleep."

"Heart of the Sea?" Blackheart muttered, tracing the inscription with a calloused finger.

The words sparked a memory in Anne's mind. One of the rumors surrounding the Spanish fort mentioned a hidden chamber, a vault named "The Heart of the Sea" where the most valuable treasures were supposedly kept.

"Could that be where we need to go?" Mary asked, her voice laced with apprehension.

Anne nodded, a flicker of hope igniting within her. The ghost had spoken of an artifact, something valuable but not necessarily gold or jewels. Perhaps the "Heart of the Sea" held the key to appeasement.

Following a barely discernible passage hidden behind a tapestry, they found themselves in a narrow tunnel that descended further into the earth. The air grew colder, and the dripping echoed louder, seemingly from all around them.

The tunnel twisted and turned, each step taking them deeper into the bowels of the fort and further from the world they knew. The silence was punctuated only by the scraping sound of their boots and the erratic beat of their hearts.

Suddenly, the passage opened into a vast cavern. Stalactites hung like menacing teeth from the ceiling, and stalagmites rose like skeletal fingers from the floor. In the center, a pool of water reflected the faint glow of their lantern, shimmering with an unnatural luminescence. This, they realized, was the "Heart of the Sea."

As they approached the pool, a low growl reverberated through the cavern, chilling them to the bone. A pair of glowing eyes emerged from the darkness, followed by a monstrous creature unlike anything they had ever seen. It resembled a giant crab, but with luminescent scales and razor-sharp claws dripping with a luminescent goo. The creature scuttled towards them, its grotesque mandibles snapping menacingly.

Panic surged through the crew. They were trapped in this subterranean chamber with a terrifying creature blocking their only escape. But Anne, her pirate spirit refusing to yield, raised her pistol and aimed.

"Stay together!" she yelled, the sound echoing through the cavern. "Fire!"

A volley of musket fire filled the air, momentarily distracting the creature. It shrieked in fury, its claws lashing out, sending a shower of rocks and debris flying.

The battle raged fiercely in the dim light. Blackheart, with his unmatched swordsmanship, parried the creature's attacks, while Mary and the others peppered it with musket fire.

Anne, however, aimed for a different target – the glowing eyes. With a well-placed shot, she plunged one of the eyes into darkness. The creature roared in pain, its movements becoming erratic.

Using this opportunity, Blackheart lunged forward and delivered a powerful blow to the creature's central carapace. It let out a final shriek before collapsing onto the cavern floor, unmoving.

Exhausted and shaken, they cautiously approached the creature's still form. In one of its claws, they found a beautifully carved obsidian amulet, its surface reflecting an otherworldly glow.

"Could this be the artifact?" Mary whispered, carefully picking it up.

Anne held the amulet, its chill seeping into her bones. It felt heavy, not with gold, but with a strange, almost sentient energy. Whether it was the answer they sought, she didn't know. But it was their only lead.

With the creature vanquished and the amulet secured, they knew it was time to return. The ascent back up the tunnel was long and arduous, but their steps were lighter, fueled by a sliver of hope. They had faced their fears, fought a monstrous guardian, and emerged with a potential key to appease the restless spirit. As they finally emerged from the trapdoor back into the treasure chamber, they found the remaining crew haggard but unharmed.

Relief washed over Anne as she surveyed them. Though shaken, they were all alive. Now came the true test – facing the vengeful spirit.

Placing the obsidian amulet on a chest in the center of the room, Anne cleared her throat and raised her voice. "Spirit of the fort, we have retrieved what you requested. We have faced the darkness below and emerged victorious. Will you finally rest?"

Silence followed, thick and heavy. Then, a slow breeze blew through the chamber, stirring the dust motes into a swirling vortex. The spectral figure of the Spanish soldier materialized before them, his form slightly less opaque, a hint of peace replacing the earlier fury in his spectral eyes.

He gazed at the amulet, a flicker of recognition crossing his spectral face. "The Heart of the Sea's guardian," he rasped, his voice less harsh than before. "A symbol of courage and sacrifice, not greed. You have shown you are worthy."

He reached out a skeletal hand and touched the amulet. A surge of energy pulsed through the chamber, the spectral figure shimmering with an otherworldly light. The chests in the room, once overflowing with treasure, seemed to shrink – the stolen gold and jewels returning to their rightful owners, leaving behind only a few artifacts of true value.

"The curse is lifted," the spirit declared, his voice gaining a semblance of peace. "May these remaining treasures serve as a reminder – true wealth lies not in stolen riches, but in courage and integrity."

With that, the spirit dissipated with a final grateful nod towards Anne. The chamber plunged back into darkness, but now it felt lighter, the oppressive aura lifted.

Relief washed over Anne. They had survived, not just the creature and the darkness, but the test of their own greed. Her gaze met Mary Read's, a silent understanding passing between them. They were pirates, yes, but they were also something more – a crew forged in fire and tested by a curse, forever marked by their adventure in the cursed fort.

But their journey wasn't over. They emerged from the fort, blinking in the sunlight, to find a troop of Governor Rogers' soldiers waiting for them, their expressions a mix of curiosity and suspicion.

Anne straightened her shoulders, the obsidian amulet cool against her skin. They had faced

the darkness and emerged with a strange prize
– not gold, but something far more valuable – a
story of courage, a reminder of the dangers of
greed, and perhaps, just perhaps, a
begrudging respect from the authorities they
had once defied.

As Anne squared her jaw and faced the
soldiers, the rising sun cast a long shadow
behind her, a symbol of the trials they had
overcome and the uncertain path that lay
ahead. Their adventure with the cursed fort
was over, but the legend of Anne Bonny, the
pirate queen who defied the odds and faced
the darkness, was just beginning.

Chapter 17

The governor's soldiers, led by a stern-faced Captain Crawford, approached with a mix of apprehension and curiosity. The rumors of a monstrous creature guarding the fort had reached Nassau, adding a layer of myth to Anne's already daring story.

"Captain Bonny," Crawford said, his voice clipped. "Governor Rogers requests your immediate presence. He wishes to hear about your… expedition."

Anne, her heart pounding but her face a mask of defiance, handed the obsidian amulet to Blackheart. "Hold onto this," she murmured. "It might prove useful."

With Mary by her side and the remaining crew trailing behind, Anne followed Crawford towards the Governor's mansion. The streets of Nassau, once teeming with pirates, now held a tense silence. The news of their success, tinged with whispers of a cursed fort and a valiant battle, had spread like wildfire.

Governor Rogers, his face etched with displeasure, sat behind his imposing desk. The air in his office crackled with barely concealed hostility.

"Captain Bonny," he began, his voice dripping with disdain. "You have returned. Alive, surprisingly."

Anne met his gaze head-on. "Alive, Governor," she corrected. "And victorious. We subdued the creature guarding the stronghold and retrieved some… artifacts." She gestured to Blackheart, who presented the amulet.

Rogers eyed the amulet with suspicion, then turned to a wizened scholar standing by his side. "Professor Eldridge, can you shed some light on this… trinket?"

Professor Eldridge examined the amulet with keen interest. "An interesting piece, Governor. Obsidian, carved in a style reminiscent of ancient Mayan rituals. It seems to hold… protective properties."

Rogers' lips pursed. He couldn't deny the strange aura emanating from the amulet. It wasn't the gold or jewels he'd expected, but it held a value beyond mere monetary worth.

"Very well," he finally conceded, a begrudging note creeping into his voice. "You have fulfilled your part of the bargain. The curse is lifted, and the remaining artifacts can be considered a reward for your services."

Anne felt a flicker of triumph, quickly extinguished by the knowledge that this was a far cry from a true pardon. They were still pirates, albeit sanctioned ones, forever teetering on the edge of legality.

"However," Rogers continued, his voice hardening, "your past transgressions cannot be ignored. You will be stripped of your captaincy, and your crew will be dispersed among the Royal Navy ships."

A wave of anger washed over Anne. They had risked their lives, faced a terrifying creature, and all they received was a slap on the wrist and a forced dissolution of their hard-earned crew.

"That's not fair, Governor!" Mary protested, her voice ringing out. "We followed orders, we fought bravely—"

Rogers silenced her with a raised hand. "Fairness has little place in these matters, Miss Read. You are pirates, and pirates must face the consequences of their actions."

Anne squared her shoulders, her defiance refusing to be cowed. "We may not be sailing together anymore," she declared, her voice steady, "but we are not broken. We will find our way, even under this… arrangement."

Rogers regarded her with a mixture of annoyance and grudging respect. This woman, this pirate captain, possessed a fire he couldn't fully extinguish.

He dismissed them with a curt nod. "Leave Nassau within the week. Consider this your final reprieve."

As they walked out into the bustling streets, a bittersweet feeling settled over Anne. They had escaped the gallows, but their freedom was shackled. They were no longer pirates, not truly, but outcasts forever marked by their adventures.

Mary, sensing Anne's dejection, squeezed her arm. "We'll find a way, Captain. We always do."

Anne looked around at the crew, their faces etched with disappointment but also a fierce loyalty. They weren't just a crew anymore; they were a band of survivors, bound by shared experiences and an audacious spirit.

Their escape from the cursed fort had brought them a hollow victory. Yet, as Anne gazed at the setting sun painting the sky in hues of orange and red, a spark of defiance ignited within her. Their story was far from over. They might be scattered, but the legend of Anne Bonny, the pirate queen who defied curses and defied authority, would continue to echo in the tales whispered on the salty winds of the Caribbean.

Years later, fate would deal Anne a cruel hand. Separated from Mary, she was eventually captured by the infamous Captain Judas. Tried and convicted of piracy, she was sentenced to hang. However, history records a final act of defiance. Pregnant at the time of her sentencing, Anne was granted a reprieve until after giving birth.

What became of Anne Bonny after her reprieve remains shrouded in mystery. Some accounts suggest she faded into obscurity, perhaps raising her child in a quiet corner of the colonies. Others whisper of a daring escape, a final act of rebellion that allowed her to disappear into the vastness of the Caribbean, her legend forever etched in pirate lore.

The truth, like the fate of Mary Read, is lost to the sands of time. But one thing remains certain: Anne Bonny, the fiery pirate queen who defied curses and defied authority, left an indelible mark on the history of piracy. Her story, a testament to courage, defiance, and the enduring allure of freedom on the open seas, continues to inspire and intrigue centuries later.

The Legend: Demystified

94

Early Life

Early Life (Uncertain Dates): A Shrouded Past

Anne Bonny's early years are as shrouded in mystery as the fate that befell her later in life. Historians have pieced together a fragmented narrative, relying on court records, hearsay, and even a touch of romanticization. While the exact details remain elusive, several competing theories paint a picture of a rebellious spirit yearning for adventure.

Irish Roots and a Scandalous Birth (1697?)

The most widely accepted theory places Anne's birth in Cork, Ireland, sometime around 1697. Her father, William Cormac, was a lawyer, a respected profession that clashed with the scandal surrounding Anne's arrival. Her mother, Mary Brennan, was William's servant. Their relationship, likely romantic in nature, resulted in Anne's illegitimate birth, a social stain in the rigid hierarchy of 18th-century Ireland.

A Life on the Fringes (Uncertain Location)

The details of Anne's childhood are hazy. Some accounts suggest William, desperate to shield his daughter from societal disapproval, raised her as a boy, dressing her in breeches and teaching her swordsmanship. This unorthodox upbringing may have fueled Anne's rebellious spirit and nurtured her desire for a life outside societal constraints.

Escape to the Colonies (Early 1700s)

William's attempts at maintaining a facade crumbled when his wife discovered Anne's true identity. Public scorn and financial constraints likely drove the family to seek a fresh start in the American colonies. Charleston, South Carolina, a burgeoning port city with a more relaxed social fabric, became their new home.

A Father's Disapproval and a Blossoming Rebellion (1710s)

Life in Charleston offered a degree of anonymity, but tensions within the family simmered. William, a traditional man, likely disapproved of Anne's adventurous spirit and unconventional ways. Accounts suggest he attempted to arrange a marriage for her with a local man, a prospect Anne vehemently rejected.

This clash of wills, coupled with the allure of a life on the open seas, may have led Anne to make a life-altering decision. In her teenage years, she is believed to have met and married James Bonny, a small-time pirate. This act of defiance marked the beginning of Anne's foray into the world of piracy, a world that promised freedom, adventure, and a chance to forge her own destiny.

The Mystery Lingers

While the details of Anne Bonny's early life remain shrouded in uncertainty, these fragments paint a picture of a young woman yearning for adventure and unwilling to be confined by societal expectations. The exact details of her escape from a life on land and her embrace of a pirate's fate remain tantalizingly out of reach, adding another layer of intrigue to the legend of Anne Bonny.

Turning to Piracy

Turning to Piracy (Early 1720s): A Life Unmoored

Anne Bonny's descent into piracy wasn't a sudden plunge but a gradual slide down a slippery slope, fueled by a restless spirit, a thirst for adventure, and a society that offered her few options.

A Rebellious Streak Simmering Beneath the Surface

Life in South Carolina, particularly for a young woman with an unconventional upbringing, couldn't contain Anne's restless spirit. The societal expectations of domesticity and submission chafed at her. Rumors swirled about her rebellious streak – tales of her dressing in men's clothing, defying authority, and harboring a fierce independence.

An Escape with a Shadowy Figure

The exact details remain hazy, but sometime in the early 1720s, Anne's life took a dramatic turn. She fled South Carolina, possibly with a sailor named James Bonny (marriage records exist, but their validity is debated). Some historians believe this was a convenient arrangement, a marriage of convenience allowing her to escape societal constraints and embrace a more adventurous life at sea.

The Lure of Calico Jack's Crew

The Bahamas, a haven for pirates like Calico Jack Rackham, beckoned. Anne, drawn to the freedom and camaraderie offered by pirate life, found herself gravitating towards Rackham's crew. Here, she could shed the limitations imposed by her gender and forge a new identity, one defined by her own strength and skills.

Disguised as a Man: A Life Reimagined

To navigate the male-dominated world of piracy, Anne took on a male persona. She donned men's clothing, learned to handle weapons with surprising skill, and cultivated a fierce demeanor. Her fiery spirit, however, wasn't completely masked. Accounts mention her sharp wit, her leadership qualities, and her ability to command respect amongst the crew.

Finding a Sister in Arms: The Unlikely Bond with Mary Read

An unexpected friendship blossomed on board Rackham's ship. Mary Read, another woman who had spent years living disguised as a man, became Anne's confidante and closest ally. They shared not just the hardships of pirate life but also a deep understanding of the constraints they had defied. Their bond, a testament to female solidarity in a brutal world, would become a defining aspect of Anne's story.

A Spark of Romance: Love Amidst the Chaos

Whether drawn together by their shared experiences or a genuine romantic connection, Anne and Rackham developed a relationship. The exact nature remains ambiguous, but it challenged the hierarchical structure of a typical pirate ship and caused friction with some crew members.

From Stowaway to Fearsome Pirate: Anne's Rise

Anne quickly proved her worth. She was a skilled fighter, a fearless leader, and a source of inspiration for others. Her reputation grew, and she became an integral part of Rackham's crew, her name whispered alongside his in taverns and on the docks.

Anne Bonny's transformation from a restless young woman to a formidable pirate wasn't an overnight occurrence. It was a journey fueled by rebellion, a yearning for adventure, and the necessity of forging her own path in a world that refused to accept her on its own terms. As

she sailed the Caribbean with Calico Jack, her
legend was just beginning to take shape.

THE REVENGE

The Revenge and the Rise to Notoriety (1720)

The Caribbean Sea in 1720 was a pirate's playground. Ships laden with gold and other treasures sailed under the watchful eyes of various empires, but none could truly control the vast expanse of blue. It was in this volatile environment that Anne Bonny, disguised as a man and fueled by a thirst for adventure, found herself aboard the vessel captained by the notorious Calico Jack Rackham.

A Rising Star Aboard the Revenge

Their initial meeting remains shrouded in mystery, but it's clear that Anne, with her fiery spirit and unwavering courage, quickly earned the respect of the crew, even the hardened pirates accustomed to a life of violence and debauchery. Her skill with a pistol and sword was undeniable, and her unwavering loyalty to Calico Jack sparked rumors of a budding romance.

A Mutiny and a New Captain

However, the crew wasn't exactly a picture of harmony. Charles Vane, the previous captain known for his brutality, still held influence. Tensions rose, culminating in a dramatic mutiny led by Anne and Mary Read, another woman disguised as a man who had become Anne's closest confidante. Vane was marooned on a deserted island, and the "Revenge" sailed on under the command of Calico Jack, with Anne Bonny emerging as a powerful figure by his side.

A Reign of Terror and Notoriety

The Caribbean trembled under the black flag of the Revenge. Anne, her red hair a fiery beacon in battle, fought alongside the crew with unparalleled ferocity. Tales of her disregard for danger and her unwavering skill spread like wildfire. Ships were plundered, not just for riches, but for a sense of rebellion against the established order. They reveled in their notoriety, becoming a thorn in the side of every governor and naval commander.

A Formidable Duo: Anne and Mary

Anne wasn't alone in her rise to infamy. Mary Read, disguised as a man named Mark, became her equal partner in crime. Their friendship blossomed into a deep bond, a fierce loyalty that fueled their defiance. Rumors of a romantic relationship between the two women only added to the legend. The sight of two women holding their own amongst the hardened pirates of the Caribbean was a source of fascination and fear.

Blackbeard's Shadow

The pirate world of the Caribbean was a web of alliances and rivalries. The infamous Blackbeard, a towering figure of brutality and legend, crossed paths with Calico Jack and his crew. A temporary alliance was forged, the two pirate ships sailing together for a time. While Blackbeard's shadow loomed large, Anne and Mary continued to carve their own path, their exploits becoming the stuff of whispers in taverns and ports throughout the islands.

The Seeds of Downfall

Despite their victories and growing reputation, trouble brewed on the horizon. The authorities were determined to quell the pirate menace, and the bounty on Calico Jack's head grew ever larger. Their reckless lifestyle and disregard for authority would eventually lead them down a perilous path, but for the time being, Anne Bonny, the fiery pirate queen, reigned supreme on the Revenge, her defiance a challenge to the established order and a testament to the power of human spirit, even on the lawless seas.

THE CURSE

The Cursed Fort and a Deal with the Devil (1720)

The Spanish fort, shrouded in perpetual mist, loomed on the horizon like a skeletal sentinel guarding a forgotten treasure. Governor Rogers' map, their dubious ticket to freedom, had led them here. But as Anne Bonny and her crew approached the crumbling ramparts, a sense of unease settled in their gut. This was no ordinary fort; it reeked of a past steeped in violence and despair.

Whispers of a Curse

Tales of a vengeful spirit guarding the fort's riches had been dismissed as pirate lore. But as they ventured deeper, the whispers seemed to solidify, chilling the air with an unseen dread. Skeletons, bleached white by the sun, sat slumped against the walls, their empty sockets like accusing stares. The silence was heavy, broken only by the echoing groans of the wind and the nervous coughs of the crew.

A Grisly Discovery

Reaching the treasure chamber, their spirits momentarily rose. Chests overflowing with gold coins, shimmering jewels, and priceless artifacts awaited them. But the air grew thick with a strange energy, and a spectral moan filled the room. A ghostly figure, clad in faded Spanish garb, materialized, its face contorted in a mask of fury and despair. It clutched a chest to its spectral form, its eyes fixated on Redbeard, who had lunged towards the treasure with avarice gleaming in his eyes.

The Price of Greed

The ghost spoke, its voice a raspy echo. This treasure, it declared, was earned with blood and sweat, not for the taking by greedy pirates. An unsettling truth settled over Anne – this was no ordinary hoard. It was cursed, bound to the restless spirit of its former guardian.

A Test of Courage

However, the ghost offered a glimmer of hope. A descent into the darkness below, a test of courage and not just greed, might appease the vengeful spirit. Failure, it warned, would condemn them to join the ranks of the restless dead.

Anne, ever the pragmatist, saw a solution. This wasn't just about treasure anymore; it was a chance to escape the clutches of the curse and the Governor's wrath. She met the ghost's gaze head-on, accepting the challenge. Only half the crew would remain to guard the treasure, while Anne, Blackheart, and a handful of brave volunteers, including the fiery Mary Read, would venture into the unknown depths.

The Heart of the Sea

The descent was a suffocating journey. Damp air clung to their skin, and the only sounds were their ragged breaths and the scraping of their boots on rough stone steps. Finally, they reached a vast, cavernous chamber – the "Heart of the Sea." An eerie luminescence emanated from a pool in the center, and a monstrous creature unlike anything they had ever seen, a luminescent crab with razor-sharp claws, emerged from the shadows.

A Battle in the Darkness

A fierce battle ensued. Blackheart, with his unmatched swordsmanship, parried the creature's attacks. Mary and the others peppered it with musket fire, while Anne aimed for a more strategic target - the glowing eyes. With a well-placed shot, she plunged the creature into darkness. Blackheart delivered a final blow, silencing the monstrous guardian.

The Offering and a Lifted Curse

In the creature's claw, they found their prize – a beautifully carved obsidian amulet, pulsating with an otherworldly glow. As they ascended back to the treasure chamber, they braced themselves for the reaction of the spirit.

Placing the amulet on a chest, Anne called out to the ghost. They had faced the darkness below, fought the guardian, and emerged victorious. Their courage, not their greed, had been tested.

A slow breeze swept through the chamber, and the spectral figure of the Spanish soldier materialized, his form less opaque, a hint of peace replacing the earlier fury. He reached out and touched the amulet, understanding dawning on his spectral face. The curse, he declared, was lifted.

A Moral Victory and a Strange Reward

The remaining chests no longer overflowed with stolen riches. A sense of balance had been restored. The true wealth, the spirit had hinted, lay not in stolen gold, but in courage and integrity.

With the curse lifted and a strange artifact in their possession, Anne knew their journey was far from over. They had faced darkness and emerged with a moral victory, not a pirate's bounty. As they emerged from the fort, blinking in the sunlight, they knew a new legend had begun - the legend of Anne Bonny, the pirate queen who defied a curse and dared to challenge the darkness.

Facing Authority

Facing Authority and a Pyrrhic Victory (1720)

Anne Bonny, ever the strategist, knew returning to Nassau wouldn't be a triumphant homecoming. Governor Rogers, a staunch opponent of piracy, loomed large, his disapproval a storm cloud on the horizon. Yet, she had a plan – a gamble on the Governor's pragmatism and a desperate hope for some semblance of freedom.

A Return with Mixed Emotions

The once-proud Revenge limped into Nassau harbor, a stark contrast to the swaggering pirate ship it had been. The crew, a motley bunch of hardened pirates and reluctant recruits, mirrored the ship's disheveled state. Some, like Mary Read, Anne's closest confidante, held a flicker of defiance in their eyes. Others, particularly the ever-grumbling Redbeard, simmered with resentment, forced to return to the very authorities they'd spent their lives evading.

A Tense Audience with the Governor

Governor Rogers, a man of ironclad resolve, received them with a mixture of suspicion and grudging respect. The rumors of a cursed island and a valiant battle against a monstrous guardian had reached Nassau, adding a layer of myth to Anne's already daring story.

Anne, her heart pounding but her voice steady, presented their case. They had faced the darkness within the fort, appeased the restless spirit, and lifted the curse. They had fulfilled their bargain, she argued, and deserved some form of leniency.

The Bargaining Chip: A Strange Artifact

Blackheart, at Anne's silent signal, stepped forward and presented the Governor with the obsidian amulet retrieved from the depths of the fort. The artifact, with its strange aura and unsettling beauty, piqued Rogers' curiosity. Professor Eldridge, a scholar summoned for the occasion, confirmed its potential for possessing protective properties.

This unexpected turn of events presented an opportunity. The Governor, ever pragmatic, saw a potential use for the amulet beyond its monetary value. It could be a symbol of his authority, a tangible reminder of the consequences of defying him.

A Pyrrhic Victory

Rogers, after a tense silence, finally spoke. He acknowledged their success in lifting the curse, a concession Anne knew came grudgingly. However, their past transgressions as pirates could not be ignored. Their captaincy would be revoked, and the crew would be dispersed amongst the Royal Navy ships.

A wave of anger washed over Anne. They had risked their lives, faced a terrifying creature, and all they received was a slap on the wrist and a forced dissolution of their hard-earned crew. Mary, ever fiery, voiced their frustration, but Rogers silenced her with a gesture.

Anne, despite the bitterness gnawing at her, refused to break. "We may not be sailing together anymore," she declared, her voice ringing with defiance, "but we are not broken. We will find our way, even under this… arrangement."

A Shaken Crew, an Uncertain Future

The crew, their faces etched with disappointment and a simmering anger, shuffled out of the Governor's mansion. The victory they had envisioned felt hollow. They were no longer pirates, not truly, but outcasts forever marked by their adventures.

Despite the harsh terms, a sliver of hope remained. They were alive. They had faced a Governor known for his ruthlessness and emerged with their lives, albeit not their freedom. As they walked out into the bustling streets of Nassau, a bittersweet feeling settled over Anne. Their adventure may have reached a turning point, but their story, the story of Anne Bonny, the pirate queen who defied curses and

defied authority, was far from over. The legend
they had forged in fire and darkness would
continue to echo in the years to come.

Uncertain Fate

Uncertain Fate (1720 onwards):
A Pirate's Ghost in the Historical Fog

The year 1720 marked a turning point for Anne Bonny. Separated from her crew and stripped of her captaincy, she vanished from the official records, leaving behind a trail of whispers and speculation. Historians have debated her fate for centuries, with several tantalizing theories emerging from the historical fog.

The Charleston Whisper (1720s - 1780s)

One theory suggests Anne returned to her roots in Charleston, South Carolina. Here, amidst the bustling port city, a flicker of hope emerges. Local records from the 1730s mention an "Ann Bonny" who died around 1782. Could this be the missing piece of the puzzle?

However, skepticism abounds. Historical evidence for this Anne Bonny is scarce, and the name itself was relatively common during that period. Was this the daring pirate queen, or simply another woman sharing a common name?

The Allure of Escape (Uncertain Date)

Another possibility, far more romanticized, paints a picture of Anne engineering a daring escape. Perhaps a loyal member of her former crew, or a sympathetic guard, aided her flight. With the Caribbean as her cloak, she could have vanished into the network of pirate havens and hidden coves, her legend continuing to grow amongst those who defied authority on the high seas.

The allure of this theory lies in its adherence to the image of Anne Bonny – a woman who defied expectations and carved her own path. Yet, the absence of any concrete evidence – escape plans, sightings, or eyewitness accounts – casts a shadow of doubt.

Lost in the Sands of Time (18th Century Onwards)

As the 18th century wore on, the details surrounding Anne Bonny's life faded further into obscurity. No official records document her capture, escape, or later life. Perhaps she died an anonymous death, her story buried with her bones in some unmarked grave.

The Legacy of Mystery

Whether Anne Bonny ended her days quietly in Charleston or vanished into the pirate underworld, her story remains captivating. Her disappearance fuels speculation, adding another layer of legend to her already remarkable life. The absence of a definitive conclusion allows her story to transcend the boundaries of history, becoming a timeless tale of defiance and the allure of a life on the fringes.

The Pirate Queen's Enduring Influence

Anne Bonny's impact goes beyond the mystery surrounding her death. She defied societal norms, embraced a life of adventure on the high seas, and challenged the male-dominated world of piracy. Her legacy serves as an inspiration for those who dare to break the mold and carve their own path.

A Spark for Further Exploration

The mystery of Anne Bonny's fate continues to tantalize historians and pirate enthusiasts alike. While the definitive answer might remain lost to time, her story serves as a spark for further exploration. Examining local records, delving into pirate lore, and analyzing the historical context of the Caribbean during this period might yield new clues.

Even without a concrete ending, Anne Bonny's life remains a testament to the power of human spirit, the allure of adventure, and the enduring fascination with pirates who defied the norms and carved their names in the annals of history.

Legacy

The Enduring Legacy of Anne Bonny

Anne Bonny's life, a whirlwind of defiance and adventure, transcended the boundaries of her time. Though her suspected demise shrouded her final chapter in mystery, her legacy continues to inspire and captivate centuries later.

A Symbol of Female Empowerment

In a world dominated by men, Anne Bonny carved her own path. She defied societal expectations, embracing a life of piracy and challenging the notion of a woman's role. Her image, wielding a cutlass and fighting alongside men, became a symbol of female empowerment for generations to come. Writers and artists found inspiration in her story, portraying her as a fearless pirate captain and a champion for those who dared to break the mold.

A Spark in the Pirate Mythos

The Golden Age of Piracy was a period of romanticized lawlessness, a time when pirates captured the imagination of the public. Anne Bonny's story added a unique spark to this mythology. Her exploits, alongside Mary Read, shattered the stereotype of the pirate as a gruff, bearded man. Their bravery and skill in battle challenged preconceived notions and added a layer of complexity to the pirate narrative.

A Reminder of Human Spirit

Anne Bonny's story resonates because it speaks to the enduring human spirit. It's a testament to facing adversity, defying authority, and carving one's own destiny. Even in her capture and forced assimilation into the Royal Navy, Anne's spirit remained unbroken. Her story serves as a reminder of the strength we possess and the resilience we can find in the face of overwhelming odds.

A Subject of Ongoing Debate

The mystery surrounding Anne Bonny's final days continues to fuel speculation and debate. Was she a quiet housewife in Charleston, or did she orchestrate a daring escape and vanish into the Caribbean? The lack of definitive answers keeps her story alive, inviting exploration and interpretation.

A Legacy Beyond History

Anne Bonny's legacy extends beyond the realm of historical accounts. She has become a cultural icon, appearing in novels, movies, video games, and even songs. Her image continues to be used in advertising campaigns, symbolizing strength, independence, and a refusal to conform.

A Call to Action

Perhaps the most potent aspect of Anne Bonny's legacy is the call to action it embodies. Her story encourages us to question the status quo, to challenge norms, and to pursue our own adventures, whatever form they may take. It's a reminder that even the most seemingly ordinary life can hold the potential for extraordinary experiences.

Anne Bonny, the pirate queen, may have faded from the pages of history, but her legend continues to burn bright. Her story serves as a testament to the power of human spirit, the allure of adventure, and the enduring pursuit of freedom. It's a legacy that will likely continue to inspire and spark imaginations for generations to come.

www.ingramcontent.com/pod-product-compliance
Lightning Source LLC
Chambersburg PA
CBHW051215160726
47994CB00002B/615